This Book
Belongs To:

....

....

FIVE-MINUTE TALES
for
FOUR
Year Olds

FIVE-MINUTE TALES
for
FOUR
Year Olds

A beautiful collection of original stories

p

Illustrated by Claire Henley

(Elizabeth Roy Literary Agency)

Language consultant: Betty Root

This is a Parragon book
This edition published in 2006

Parragon
Queen Street House
4 Queen Street
Bath BA1 1HE, UK

ISBN 1-40546-955-2

Printed in China

Contents

Rocky Finds a New Job

Nick Ellsworth

"Hooray! It's Saturday!" yelled Tom and Jenny as they ran out of the house. They rushed towards the park, dragging Mum with them. They ran straight up to the little café, where Rocky the Dinosaur sold ice creams.

Everyone liked Rocky. He was always happy, and loved all the children.

"Hello, Tom! Hello, Jenny!" grinned Rocky.

"Can we have two orange lollies, please?" they asked.

"Of course you can," said Rocky, reaching into the big fridge.

"We're going on the roundabout now. See you later, Rocky," said Tom. Jenny sat on the roundabout, while Tom started to push.

"Don't go too fast," said Jenny. "I'll get dizzy."

"Don't worry," said Tom. "Just hold on tight."

"Wheee," they yelled excitedly, as they spun round.

Next, the two children played pirates on the climbing frame. As they started to climb, Mr Gribble the park keeper walked up with a big sign that said, "KEEP OFF!"

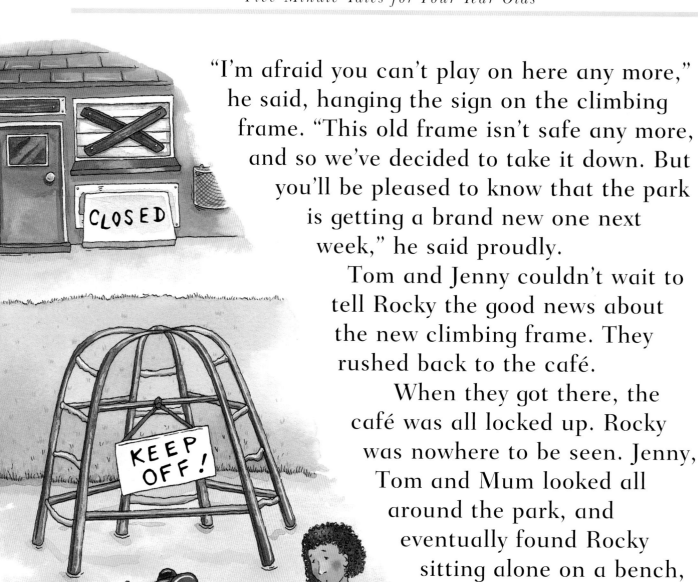

"I'm afraid you can't play on here any more," he said, hanging the sign on the climbing frame. "This old frame isn't safe any more, and so we've decided to take it down. But you'll be pleased to know that the park is getting a brand new one next week," he said proudly.

Tom and Jenny couldn't wait to tell Rocky the good news about the new climbing frame. They rushed back to the café.

When they got there, the café was all locked up. Rocky was nowhere to be seen. Jenny, Tom and Mum looked all around the park, and eventually found Rocky sitting alone on a bench, looking miserable.

"Are you all right, Rocky?" they asked.

"I'm afraid I don't have a job any more," said Rocky sadly.

"Why?" asked the children.

"Well, the new climbing frame is very expensive. There's not enough money to buy it and keep the café open as well. So I have to look for a new job," replied Rocky, looking even sadder.

"We'll miss you so much," said Jenny, almost crying.

Rocky gave her a hug, and told her that he'd come and visit her soon.

"Poor Rocky," said Tom, as they watched him walk slowly out of the park.

As Rocky passed the local museum, he saw a sign:

"Dinosaur Wanted. Apply Within."

"Can I have a job, please?" he asked, walking up to the front entrance.

"Of course you can!" said the museum keeper brightly. "All you have to do is stand in a room all day, and let all the people stare at you."

"That doesn't sound much fun," thought Rocky. "But I'll give it a go, anyway."

Later that week, Tom and Jenny persuaded their big brother Ben to take them to the park. The new climbing frame was coming that very afternoon.

All the children were looking forward to playing on the new frame, but at the same time they were sad that Rocky wasn't there to join in the excitement.

All of a sudden, Mr Gribble came rushing up.

"Something terrible has happened!" he said.

"What's wrong?" asked Tom and Jenny.

"I've just heard that the new climbing frame has fallen apart. It's completely useless! Everyone will be so upset!" he said unhappily.

Just then, Tom had an idea. He grabbed Jenny and Ben by the hand.

"Back in a minute," he shouted, and they all ran out of the park.

They raced into town, and ran straight into the museum. They found Rocky standing very still in one of the rooms. It was so quiet you could hear a pin drop. There were lots of very serious looking people all staring at him.

Rocky's eyes lit up when he saw Tom and Jenny. He was so pleased to see his friends.

"Hello, Tom! Hello, Jenny!" he exclaimed. "What are you doing here?"

"We've come to visit you," said Tom. "Do you like working here, Rocky?"

"It's all right, I suppose," said Rocky. "It's not as much fun as working in the park. All I do is stand here all day while people look at me."

"Come with us!" said Tom, quickly grabbing Rocky's hand. They ran out of the museum.

"Where are we going?" cried Rocky.

"You'll see," said Tom, as they went back to the park.

There, the children ran straight up to Mr Gribble.

"I've had a great idea!" said Tom. "Why can't Rocky be our new climbing frame?"

"Well… I don't know," said Mr Gribble, scratching his head.

"Oh, please," cried Jenny. "It's a brilliant idea, and will make everyone so happy." They waited for his answer, hardly daring to breathe.

"I think it's a wonderful idea, too," said Mr Gribble, finally. "Welcome back, Rocky!"

Everyone cheered as loudly as they could, especially Tom and Jenny.

"I'm the luckiest dinosaur in the world," said Rocky, as the children climbed and played on him all day long.

Mollie and Moonlight

Ronne Randall

Of all her toys, Mollie's favourite was her little horse, Moonlight. She was pale silver, and her eyes sparkled like stars. Moonlight sat on the window-sill in Mollie's bedroom.

Mollie and Moonlight had wonderful pretend adventures. Together they rode through magical forests, climbed snowy mountains and raced across hot deserts. They fought dragons, captured robbers and rescued lost lambs in the wild.

Mollie loved Moonlight. But more than anything, she wished that Moonlight could be a real pony, who would prance and gallop and take her on real adventures. Mollie's mum and dad told her that they couldn't have a real pony where they lived.

"Ponies need room to run and race about," said Mum. "We only have a little garden."

Even so, every night before she went to bed, Mollie looked up to see if the Wishing Star was out. If it was, she would look up at it and whisper:

I wish I may,
I wish I might
Have a REAL LIVE pony
Like Moonlight!

One night, not long after Mollie fell asleep, a soft whooshing noise woke her up. She sat up in bed and saw that her window was open, and the wind was blowing the curtain. The moon was shining into Mollie's bedroom.

In the shimmering moonlight, Mollie noticed something that made her heart stop – Moonlight was gone! But high in the sky, the Wishing Star was winking and twinkling down at her, almost as if it was calling her to the window.

Jumping out of bed, Mollie rushed to the window and looked out. She could hardly believe her eyes! There, prancing around the apple tree in the middle of the garden, was Moonlight. She was as big and alive as could be. Moonlight looked up.

"Come and play with me, Mollie," she called softly.

Filled with wonder and excitement, Mollie rushed downstairs. She let herself out of the back door and ran into the garden.

"You're alive!" she cried, jumping on Moonlight's back. "And you can talk!"

"It's the magic of the Wishing Star," said Moonlight. "At every full moon, the Wishing Star Fairy grants one person's wish for just one night. Tonight it's your turn!"

With Mollie on her back, Moonlight trotted around the garden. Then she began to gallop and, with a quick leap, sailed over the garden fence.

Mollie held her breath and clung to Moonlight's silver mane as they galloped through all the gardens in the street. The wind ruffled her hair, and Mollie had never been so happy in her life.

Suddenly, it felt as if Moonlight was galloping on the wind itself. Looking down, Mollie realized that they were flying in the wind, springing up, up, up, high into the midnight sky.

"Where are we going?" she asked Moonlight.

"You'll see," Moonlight replied.

Higher and higher they flew, high above the rooftops and treetops. The full moon cast its silvery beams, and all around them the stars twinkled merrily. But one star shone more brightly than all the others.

"It's the Wishing Star!" gasped Mollie.

"Yes," said Moonlight. "And we're going to visit it."

As they got closer, Mollie saw that the Wishing Star was really a big, shining throne. On it sat a beautiful fairy with long, sparkling hair and a twinkling wand made of silver and stardust.

"I am the Wishing Star Fairy," she told Mollie. "I hear all the wishes that are made to the Wishing Star, and I decide which ones will come true."

"Why did you choose mine?" asked Mollie.

"Because I know how much you love Moonlight," the Wishing Star Fairy explained, "and love always helps to make things real. So yours was an easy wish to grant. But it will only be true for tonight. In the morning, Moonlight will be a toy horse again."

"I know," said Mollie, "but I will love her just as much."

"Then she
will always be real to you,"
said the fairy. "Now, go and enjoy your adventures!"

With a prance, Moonlight took Mollie swooping
through the stars and clouds. They leapt over moonbeams,
darted between shooting stars and raced around planets.
All the while, the Wishing Star Fairy watched, smiling,
from her starry throne.

When the first light of dawn began painting the sky
pink, Mollie knew it was time to go home.

She held on tightly as Moonlight flew her back down, over the garden and in through her bedroom window. Tired and happy, Mollie crawled into bed, and in seconds she was fast asleep.

Soon sunlight was streaming through the window, and Mollie's mum was calling from downstairs.

"Mollie, it's time to get up!"

Mollie looked over at the window-sill. There was Moonlight, just where she always was.

"Was I just dreaming?" Mollie wondered. She rushed to the window and looked down into the garden.

Everything looked the same, but... were those really hoofprints around the apple tree? Mollie looked at Moonlight, whose eyes were twinkling merrily. Maybe it was the breeze blowing Moonlight's mane, or maybe Mollie's eyes were playing tricks on her. But she was sure Moonlight was gently nodding at her!

Dance Jiggle, Dance!

Jan Payne

All the animals at Windy Farm are getting a bit fed up. The problem is Jiggle the donkey. He is dancing again! They can hear him from inside the barn. He has put music on and he is tap-dancing.

Tappa-tappa-tap. Tappa-tappa-tap.

It's a sunny afternoon and the animals are looking forward to some peace and quiet. But thanks to Jiggle that's not going to happen. Constance the cat wanders over to the barn to have a word with Jiggle.

"Hey, Jiggle!" she calls. "Must you do that now?"

"Yes, I must," answers Jiggle. He is using an old fallen-down door as a stage. Jiggle loves the sound his hooves make as he tap-dances on the hard wood.

Tappa-tappa-tap. Tappa-tappa-tap.

Jiggle loves to dance. He has read in the local paper about a dancing competition, and he is determined to win. But first he has to find a partner.

Jiggle goes over to the pond to ask Duck. She listens politely, her head on one side.

"I'd like to help, Jiggle," says Duck, "but I've got flat feet."

Next, Jiggle goes to the sty to ask Pig. He snorts with laughter. "You've got to be joking," says Pig. "If I dance with you, everyone will laugh at me."

Then Jiggle goes to the barn to ask Cow. She is being milked. "I can't," says Cow. "If I jig about my milk gets too frothy."

Jiggle sees a picture in his head of a milkshake in a tall glass.

"I'd like that," Jiggle says.

"But Farmer Brown wouldn't," answers Cow. "Go and ask Sheep." Sheep is standing in the shade wearing a yellow sunhat.

"Sheep," asks Jiggle, "will you dance with me in the competition next week?"

"It's much too hot to dance, Jiggle," replies Sheep, fanning herself with a large leaf. "I've got such a thick coat, I shall melt if I move quickly. Ask Hen – she can't keep still for two minutes."

"What do you want?" Hen asks Jiggle crossly, as she scratches in the dirt. Jiggle doesn't feel like asking.

"Nothing," he says, turning away. But Jiggle refuses to be put off. He practises tap-dancing in the barn every day. All the animals are getting more and more fed up with the sound of his tapping feet.

Tappa-tappa-tap.
Tappa-tappa-tap.

The day of the competition arrives. It is warm and
sunny and the village green looks very festive. There are
tents and stalls and games and lots of delicious things to
eat. Jiggle sees Duck eating an ice cream, and Pig is
almost hidden behind a huge bundle of candy floss. Big
Horse has entered the Strong Animal Competition.

From the biggest tent comes the sound of music. Jiggle looks at a board showing the names of the competitors. He is surprised to see the names of Farmer Brown and Mrs Brown. Mrs Brown is very jolly and very kind, but she is rather large with short legs. Jiggle doesn't think she will be much good at dancing.

He goes into the tent to watch. First, two pigs dance a waltz. Then, two chickens dance a tango and two cows do a break-dance. They are all very good, especially the cows.

Soon it's the turn of Farmer and Mrs Brown. All the animals cheer loudly and stamp their hooves. But, as they make their way to the stage, Farmer Brown trips over Constance the cat. He falls heavily and bangs his knee. The music starts. But Farmer Brown can't get up.

Mrs Brown looks round and sees Jiggle. "Will you be my partner?" she asks.

Will he? Jiggle can't wait to start dancing! As Mrs Brown holds his mane they walk onto the stage in the middle of the tent to loud clapping.

"Do your best, Jiggle," whispers Mrs Brown.

The pair dance superbly. Mrs Brown may be rather large with short legs, but she is quick and light on her feet. Jiggle has never danced so well, he moves like lightning across the stage and Mrs Brown keeps up with him. Their feet tap together in perfect rhythm.

Tappa-tappa-tap. Tappa-tappa-tap.

The judge has no doubts about which pair should receive the first prize. It is the happiest day of Jiggle's life.

Now the other animals don't mind Jiggle's dancing quite so much. Mrs Brown has given him some new music, and on one of them there is singing. Sometimes, Jiggle even joins in!

"I'm only a dancing donkey,
My voice may be quite honky,
But I dance and sing 'till the rafters ring
And my knees start feeling wonky!"

Whenever Jiggle starts singing, the other animals cover up their ears and yell together,

"For goodness sake, Jiggle!"

Tappa-tappa-tap. Tappa-tappa-tap.

No Such Thing as Magic

Gaby Goldsack

Joshua Smith looked like an ordinary little boy. He lived in an ordinary house, in an ordinary street, with ordinary parents.

But Joshua wasn't ordinary at all. You see, Joshua was a wizard. A wizard who could do all sorts of magical things… like turning dogs into toads, and cabbages into cakes!

Joshua was a very clever wizard indeed. But Joshua had one tiny problem.

No one, not even his parents, believed it when he told them he was a wizard. In fact, they didn't even believe in magic.

Joshua always tried his best to show his mum and dad what a wizard wizard he was. He made spells to improve his mum's cooking, and spells to help his dad fix things. But Mum and Dad were always too busy being grown-ups to take any notice. They didn't even seem to notice when some of Joshua's more unusual friends came round to play.

"Of course," smiled Mum, whenever Joshua asked if Martha the Monster or Dermot the Dragon could come round. "But do it quietly."

Joshua could tell that she thought he was being silly.

And whenever Joshua said that he was the magical wizard, who had made his mum's fairy cakes cook properly, she'd laugh,

"Joshua, don't be daft. There's no such thing as magic!"

Not even Joshua's friends believed he was a wizard. They thought he was joking. Even when he made scrummy cakes and yummy sandwiches appear for them to eat.

"Your mum must have made them," they'd laugh. They didn't know what a terrible cook Joshua's mum was.

Then, on Joshua's birthday, he had a huge party at his house. He invited all of his friends. They played lots of games. Then Mum sat them all down in front of the party food and went to have a cup of tea in the kitchen.

The children piled their plates high with food, then began to tuck in. But they soon stopped.

"Yuck!" said Charlotte, who wasn't quite as polite as the rest.

"Sorry," said Joshua, "but I've always said that my mum can't cook."

"What about all those scrummy cakes and yummy sandwiches you usually have?" said Joshua's friend Tom.

"I've told you," explained Joshua. "I make those with my magic."

"But my dad says there's no such thing as magic," said Joshua's next door neighbour, Sam.

"I'll show you," cried Joshua, throwing his arms wide open and shouting, *"Abracadabra!"*

In a flash, the dry sandwiches and soggy sausage rolls disappeared and plates were soon piled high with lots of shiny sweets, cream-filled buns and wobbly jellies. At the centre of the table stood an enormous chocolate-covered birthday cake. It was taller than they were, almost touching the ceiling. It was the biggest birthday cake anyone had ever seen.

"Yesssss!" cried all the children, tucking in greedily. And they didn't stop until every single mouthful of food had disappeared.

"Wow," burped Sam. "So you really are a wizard, after all."

"Yes," replied Joshua, looking very pleased with himself. "I've always told you I was. And to prove it even more, I'm going to bring in some of my special friends."

Joshua stood back and clapped his hands three times. In a puff of magic smoke, Martha the Monster and Dermot the Dragon appeared before them. They looked so fearsome that the children began to feel frightened.

Abracadabra!

"Don't be afraid," laughed Joshua, "Martha and Dermot are the cuddliest, friendliest, nicest creatures you could wish to meet. In fact, they're probably more afraid of you than you are of them."

And he was right, Martha and Dermot were a little afraid of the children. But, after Joshua had explained that none of them would pull their tails or tweak their ears, they crept over to say hello. Before long, everyone was getting on very well.

Dermot had a brilliant time giving the children rides around the room, and then Martha showed them all how to do the monster stomp.

Everyone squealed with laughter as they thumped around the dining room while Dermot tapped out the beat with his tail.

Then, suddenly, above all the noise, Joshua heard a door bang. His mum was coming back. Quick as a flash, he clapped his hands and Martha and Dermot disappeared. By the time the door swung open, all the children were sitting back around the table once more.

"What was all that noise about?" frowned Mum.

"Nothing," cried all the children at once.

And Mum soon forgot all about the noise when she saw their empty plates. "Brilliant," she beamed. "Looks like you all enjoyed that."

"Yes," cried Joshua and his friends. They certainly had enjoyed their magical afternoon.

And from that day on, Joshua's friends never forgot that he was an amazing wizard. But they all agreed that the grown-ups should never be told, because, after all, grown-ups think "there's no such thing as magic!"

Elephant Has a Cold

Ronne Randall

It was a peaceful morning in the jungle.

Parrot was flying through the treetops, calling "Good morning" to everyone.

Giraffe was nibbling leaves.

Monkey was picking coconuts.

Hippo was wallowing in the muddy river.

Everything was calm and quiet. Until…

AH-CHOO-BOOOOOM!

The loud crash echoed through the jungle, rattling the treetops and making the ground tremble. Coconuts toppled down and rolled everywhere.

"What happened?" cried Monkey.

"Was it an earthquake?" asked Giraffe.

"The riverbed shook!" Hippo exclaimed.

All the animals were worried that something terrible was happening in the jungle.

Then Parrot solved the mystery.

"I saw it all," she said, flying down to them. "It was Elephant. He has a cold – and he sneezed!"

Suddenly…

AH-CHOO-BOOOOOM!

It happened
again and again.
Trees shook, and large
rocks began sliding into
the river.

"This is awful!" said
Hippo, hurrying onto the bank. "We
have to do something!"

When another... AH-CHOO-BOOOOOM!
echoed through the jungle, the animals' minds were
made up.

"We have to cure Elephant's cold," said Giraffe.

"Otherwise we'll never have any peace."

Together, the animals tramped through the jungle to
Elephant's home. As they got closer, they could hear loud
sniffling and snuffling.

"Hello!" said Elephant when he saw his friends. "I hab a tode in my drunk!"

"Pardon?" said Giraffe politely.

"I think Elephant is trying to say that he has a cold in his trunk," Parrot explained.

"Oh!" said Giraffe. "We know! We heard you sneezing and we're here to help!"

"Dank oo!" said Elephant, which the others understood meant "Thank you!"

"Warm coconut milk can be very soothing," said Monkey. "I've got some fresh coconuts right here. I'll make you a nice drink."

Monkey opened a coconut, poured out some milk, and warmed it in the sunshine before giving it to Elephant. Elephant stuck out his trunk and tried to drink some of the milk.

Slip-slurp-s-s-s... AH-CHOO-BOOOOOM!
A great big sneeze sent the coconut milk flying, splashing over everyone else.

"Oh dear," said Monkey.

Elephant sniffled miserably. "I've nebber had a tode before," he said. "I dust want to feel bedder!"

"Why don't you try a nice soothing mud bath?" asked Hippo. "That always makes me feel better!"

Everyone thought that sounded like a good idea, so Elephant followed Hippo down to the river. Together they sank into the warm, muddy water.

"Berry relaxig!" said Elephant.

"Yes," said Hippo. "It is very relaxing, isn't it?" Everyone else was beginning to relax, too, as they watched Elephant sink down deeper into the mud with a happy smile on his face.

"Ahhh," sighed Elephant contentedly. "Ahhh...

ahhh...AH-CHOO-BOOOOOM!

Elephant's sneeze splattered mud all over his friends.

"It's no use," said Parrot, shaking the mud out of her feathers. "There's only one thing to do."

"What?" asked the others.

"We'll have to call Dr Lion," said Parrot. "He's the only one who will know how to cure Elephant's cold once and for all."

So Parrot flew off towards the plains, where Dr Lion lived. In the meantime, the others tried to make Elephant comfortable.

Soon Parrot was back with Dr Lion.

"Where's the patient?" Dr Lion asked importantly. The animals led him to Elephant, who was sitting miserably with some palm leaves wrapped around his trunk.

"Hmmm…" said Dr Lion, listening to Elephant's chest.

"Say ahhh," said Dr Lion, looking at Elephant's throat.

"I see," said Dr Lion, looking in Elephant's ears. "Yes, indeed," said Dr Lion, looking down Elephant's trunk.

"Well," said Dr Lion, after he had finished examining Elephant, "the only thing that will cure Elephant's bad cold is…"

The other animals came closer to listen.

"...rest!" announced Dr Lion. "Lots of rest is the only cure for a cold in the trunk."

The animals all thanked Dr Lion, and said they would make sure Elephant got as much rest as possible.

As soon as Dr Lion left, they got started. Monkey and Giraffe gathered leaves and twigs to make a cosy bed for Elephant. Hippo tucked him in, and Parrot sang him a soft lullaby. Soon Elephant was fast asleep.

Elephant slept for the rest of the day... and all that night... and all the next day and night, too.

His friends took turns sitting with him so they could be sure he was all right. He snuffled and snorted and snored, but he didn't sneeze. Not once!

On the third morning, Elephant woke up, stretched his trunk, and took a deep breath...

"Ah... ah..."

All his friends held their breath…

"…Aaaaaaahhhh! I feel SO much better!" Elephant announced.

The other animals cheered and hugged Elephant. "We're so glad!" they said.

"Thank you all for looking after me," said Elephant. "You've been such good friends. And, of course, I would do the same for you if any of you had a cold!"

"That's good," said Parrot, "because I think…

SQUAWK-CHOOOOOO!

…I may be next!"

Blossom the Cow

Tony Payne

At the top of the hill was a farm.

On the farm there was a big house,

and a stable for the horse,

and a coop for the chickens,

and a pen for the sheep,

and a sty for the pigs,

and a milking shed for Blossom the cow.

The farmer was called Mr Pinstripe, and Blossom was
his favourite animal. Farmer Pinstripe looked after
Blossom and the other animals. Mrs Pinstripe looked after
the visitors who came to stay on the farm on holiday.

One Monday morning at breakfast, Mrs Pinstripe noticed that none of her visitors had eaten their corn flakes. Then she noticed that none of them had drunk their tea or coffee, or eaten their bread and butter, or their yoghurt.

"Is anything wrong with your breakfast?" Mrs Pinstripe asked them.

"No! Not at all!" they cried. "No, absolutely not! No, no, no... well..."

"The butter tastes funny," said one of the visitors quickly. "And the yoghurt tastes funny too," said another.

"And the cream and milk taste funny," said someone else.

Mrs Pinstripe remembered that the same thing had happened last Monday. And the Monday before that. It was very odd.

"I can't understand it," she said. "Yesterday's milk was lovely. It must be that cow of yours, Blossom," she complained to Farmer Pinstripe.

Farmer Pinstripe scratched his head. He couldn't understand it either. Blossom's milk was the best he'd ever tasted. She had won prizes for it. What could be wrong? He would have to keep an eye on her. Farmer Pinstripe decided to watch Blossom wherever she went.

All that day, he watched Blossom eat grass. Sometimes he watched her annoying flies with her swishy tail, and sometimes he watched her doing nothing at all. Cows are very good at doing nothing at all!

That evening, Farmer Pinstripe led Blossom back to her shed for milking. Then he tasted the milk. It was lovely and sweet.

Farmer Pinstripe followed Blossom around again the next day. Once again all she did was eat grass until she came back in the evening to be milked.

Again, the milk tasted really lovely.

For the next few days, Farmer Pinstripe followed Blossom everywhere. He still found nothing wrong.

On Sunday, Blossom seemed excited. She almost skipped as Farmer Pinstripe let her into the field. Then, instead of going to the top field or middle field, she went straight down to the pretty stream at the bottom of the hill, and waited.

Soon, a group of children came into the field with a big blue picnic box. First they chose the best spot to sit, under a big oak tree. Then they laid a large rug on the grass. They sat down and took out paper plates and plastic cups and little plastic knives and forks. Then they took out pizza and coke and sandwiches and cake and chocolate milk and chicken...

Blossom stood close to the children, as if she was one of the gang. They made a big fuss of her, scratching her behind her ears and blowing gently on her face. Then they offered her pizza. Blossom shook her head. They put cake under her nose, but she turned her head away.

The children
showed her
all the other
things in their
picnic box, one
by one. Blossom
looked at
everything, shaking
her head, until...
she saw what she had
been waiting for.

It was the salt and vinegar crisps!

Blossom gobbled them up... and the cheese and onion crisps, and the spicy barbecue flavoured ones too. She liked everything with a strong taste!

Farmer Pinstripe was amazed. "So," he said to himself, "that's why the milk tastes so funny on Monday mornings."

When he told his wife they put their heads together and came up with a plan.

Next Sunday evening, after her picnic with the children, Farmer Pinstripe gave Blossom a handful of extra-strong peppermints. She loved them so much he let her eat the whole packet. Then he waited a while before he milked her.

On Monday morning, while the guests were eating their breakfast, Mrs Pinstripe watched carefully. She watched as they ate the corn flakes, and as they drank the milk. Then, to her delight, when they finished the yoghurts they asked for more!

The visitors ate everything. Mrs Pinstripe was very relieved. After the last visitor had left to go home, Mr and Mrs Pinstripe read their comments in the visitors' book they kept in the hall.

They had written: "We had a lovely holiday. We loved the farm and all the animals. Mrs Pinstripe looked after us very well. The food was wonderful, and especially... the peppermint-flavoured yoghurt!"

I'll Have to Think Again

Jillian Harker

Frog sat on a large lily-pad, reading a cookery book. "Flour, milk, eggs and honey," he muttered. "That shouldn't be difficult." It was Frog's birthday and he wanted to make a huge birthday cake and invite all his friends to tea. He'd never made a cake before, but he was sure it would be easy.

Of course, he needed the ingredients first. "Flour," he gulped, as he plopped into the river.

A little way
downstream was a mill.
Frog often played there, jumping from one paddle of the
wheel to the next, and he always cheered up the miller.

"The miller won't mind giving me some flour," thought
Frog, springing onto the bank.

When Frog explained what he wanted, the miller
smiled. "No problem," he grinned. "But how will you get
the flour home?"

"I'll swim up the river with it," replied Frog.

"A bag of flour will weigh you down," warned the
miller. "The flour will get wet, and it will be no use to
you at all."

"Oh!" said Frog, surprised. "I'll have to think again!"

Frog leapt back into the cool river and swam towards the meadow.

"I'll get the milk first. That shouldn't be difficult," he told himself, hopping onto the bank. Frog often went to the meadow to catch juicy flies. This helped Brown Cow, because it stopped them bothering her.

"Brown Cow won't mind giving me some milk," Frog thought. And he was right. Brown Cow mooed deeply, when Frog explained what he wanted.

"Of course you can have some milk," she told Frog, "but what will you carry it in? You have no pail and, even if you did, the milk would pour out and mix with the river water. Then it would be no use to you at all."

"Oh!" said Frog, surprised. "I'll have to think again!"

Frog slid down the river bank and set off upstream.

"Perhaps I should get the eggs first," Frog gurgled to himself, creeping onto the river bank beside the farm.

Every morning, when he got up, Frog gave an extra loud croak. This helped Speckled Hen to wake up and lay the breakfast eggs on time.

"Speckled Hen won't mind giving me some eggs," Frog told himself. And he was right. Speckled Hen didn't mind at all.

"Take as many as you need," she told Frog, "but how will you get the eggs home? You have no basket, and you need your front legs to swim."

"I'll tuck the eggs under my chin," said Frog.

"Then you'll certainly drop them," replied Speckled Hen. "Eggs break easily, and if they smash they will be no use to you at all."

"Oh! said Frog, surprised. "I'll have to think again."

Frog hopped across the farmyard, past the farmhouse and through the hedge.

"I am silly!" croaked Frog. "I should have got the honey first." He jumped down the lane to the beekeeper's cottage. Frog often helped the beekeeper by telling his bees where they could find the best flowers.

"The beekeeper won't mind giving me some honey," Frog mumbled to himself. It was true. The beekeeper was happy to give Frog some honey.

"Goody!" said Frog, holding out his web-fingered hands. "Just spoon some onto here."

"My dear friend," said the beekeeper, "I can't put honey in your hands. It'll run away. I don't think I should give you a jar either. If it drops and breaks you're sure to cut yourself, but..." Frog didn't wait for him to finish.

"It's all right," he croaked huskily, as a tear fell from the corner of his eye. "I'll just have to think again." And he limped off down the lane.

By the time he got back to the lily-pad he had no idea how he could get the ingredients for his birthday cake.

"There must be a simpler recipe than this," he thought. He dangled his tired feet in the cool water and flicked through the pages of the cookery book. He felt very miserable. The sun was warm and he was tired. Soon, he was fast asleep.

"Happy Birthday to you, Happy Birthday to you...!"

Suddenly Frog woke up. On the bank of the pond stood all his friends. And the miller was holding a huge birthday cake.

"How on earth...?" gasped Frog.

"Well," said the beekeeper, "we wanted to help you for a change. The miller brought a bag of flour, Brown Cow came in from the meadow to be milked, Speckled Hen laid some eggs and I brought a jar of honey and baked the cake."

"How very kind," said Frog quietly. "But I was going to make a cake to surprise you."

"Well," laughed his friends together, "you'll have to think again."

Elephants Don't Eat Jelly!

Tony Payne

"Mum, which day are we going to the zoo?" Jessica asked at breakfast.

"Tomorrow," said Mum.

"Is Jake coming?"

"Of course," replied Mum. Jake was Jessica's baby brother. He couldn't even walk yet. What's more he couldn't even eat properly! Jessica watched as he tipped a bowl of cereal on his head.

"I hope he doesn't do that tomorrow," she said.

Jake grinned and waved his spoon at her.

Jessica was really looking forward to going to the zoo. She loved animals and she wanted to see as many as possible. The lions, the elephants, the monkeys, the penguins, the giraffes... oh, and the anteaters. Her best friend Jane had told her that anteaters were cool! Jessica wasn't quite sure what that meant.

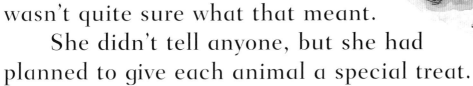

She didn't tell anyone, but she had planned to give each animal a special treat.

When they got to the zoo, their first stop was the elephants. They were standing very still in their enclosure, like enormous grey statues. Jessica looked at their huge feet, their legs like tree trunks, and their big heads with very small squinty eyes.

"What's that?" she whispered to Dad.

"That's his trunk," said Dad. "That's what he smells with."

"Like a nose?" said Jessica.

"A bit," said Dad, "but he can also pick up tiny things with it."

Jessica watched as the elephant picked a nut from the ground with the tip of his trunk and put it in his mouth.

She took her bag off her back and opened it. Then she took out a little pot of red jelly and a white plastic spoon.

"Do elephants eat jelly?" she asked, holding it up.

"No, elephants don't eat jelly," laughed Mum.

"And look," pointed Dad, "there's a notice which says PLEASE DON'T FEED THE ELEPHANTS."

Jessica put the pot of jelly back into her bag. As they moved away, the elephant began to bellow loudly. When Jessica looked round he had sucked up water with his trunk and was about to squirt them with it.

"I think he really did want the jelly!" she said.

PLEASE
DON'T FEED
THE
ELEPHANTS

They could still hear the noise when they reached the monkeys. The monkeys were crazy. Climbing trees, hanging upside down, and pulling rude faces. A baby monkey came close to Jessica and held out his hand.

Jessica opened her bag and took out a small packet. "Do monkeys eat chocolate biscuits?" she asked.

"No, monkeys don't eat chocolate biscuits," said Dad. And he pointed to a notice which said PLEASE DON'T FEED THE MONKEYS.

The baby monkey was looking at Jessica with wistful brown eyes. When she put the packet of chocolate biscuits back in her bag, he put a finger in each corner of his mouth and stretched it wide, making a silly face. Then he stuck out his tongue! Jake laughed.

"I think he really did want the chocolate biscuits," said Jessica as they moved away.

PLEASE
DON'T FEED
THE
MONKEYS

The penguins were so serious. Jessica loved them. She watched as they walked in single file round the pool. When they had walked all the way round they turned, and walked all the way back again. There was one little penguin who couldn't keep up with the rest. She smiled at him when he passed her, but he didn't smile back!

A man appeared with a bucket of fish. He threw the fish in the pool and the penguins dived in. When they were swimming they looked quite different.

They were fast and energetic, even the little penguin. When all the fish was gone and the bucket was empty Jessica went up to the man.

"Do penguins eat cheese triangles?" she inquired, holding a round box in her hands.

"No," said the man, smiling. "Penguins don't eat cheese triangles." When he moved out of the way Jessica could see the notice which said PLEASE DON'T FEED THE PENGUINS.

PLEASE
DON'T FEED
THE
PENGUINS

It was the same with the giraffes. They didn't eat barbeque flavoured crisps!

The lions didn't eat yoghurts!

The parrots didn't eat dolly mixtures!

And the ant eaters only ate ants! Jessica thought they were funny, not cool at all. Mum could see how disappointed she was.

"Never mind," she said, "we are going to have a picnic now. You can get out all the special treats, the jelly, the cheese triangles, the crisps, and feed your baby brother."

Jake grinned. He liked it when Jessica fed him. So that's what she did.

It was nearly as much fun as feeding the animals!

Ella's Playhouse

Clive Batkin

One hot summer's day, Ella found her dad snoozing in his deckchair.

"Dad," she called out. "I'd really like a playhouse in the garden. Will you build me one?" Ella's dad woke up and said sleepily, "Of course, Ella, anything you like." Then he then turned over and went straight back to sleep. After all, there was the whole summer left for doing tiring jobs like building things!

"Will it be ready by this afternoon?" asked Ella, shaking him by the arm.

"It might take me a little longer than that," said Dad.

Ella smiled and skipped happily away.

She couldn't wait to play in her new playhouse!

After an hour or so, Ella came back with some of her dolls.

"Is the playhouse finished, Dad?" she asked.

Dad, who was still in his deckchair, looked a bit surprised!

"Well, Ella, making a playhouse is not as easy as all that!" he explained. "First we'll have to draw a picture of what we want it to look like, and then..."

"That's OK, Dad. I know exactly how I want it!" said Ella. "I'll go and get my crayons."

Ella's dad sighed quietly to himself, got up out of his chair and followed Ella into the house. The pair sat round the kitchen table, with Ella's big pot of crayons and a huge pad of white paper.

After a while, they had finished the drawing of the playhouse. It had pink walls, four little windows and a bright-red front door. It also had curtains and a white fence around the outside.

"That's exactly right!" beamed Ella. "Now, when will it be ready?"

"Oh, in a little while," said Dad doubtfully, "but I think I'll need a cup of tea before I get started."

Ella went off to get some more of her toys, while Dad went into the kitchen. In a while, Ella came back and heard the kettle whistling.

"Is my house ready yet, Dad?"

Dad, who hadn't even poured milk into his tea cup yet, jumped up from his chair.

"Well, Ella, it's not as easy as all that," he explained. "I'll have to find some wood to make the walls and roof, and..."

"That's OK, Dad. There are lots of bits of wood in the shed. I'll help you get them."

Ella dragged him by the hand to the shed at the bottom of the garden. Normally Dad tried not to go into the shed because it was full of not only bits of wood, but lots of dust and spiders as well!

After an hour, they had collected enough wood. Ella's dad was now very hot, dirty, dusty and covered in cobwebs! He was also exhausted!

"I've done more than enough work for today," he

thought to himself, "and the football is about to start on the television. I don't want to miss that."

Ella's dad crept back into the house. Shutting the living room door, he turned on the television and settled himself on the sofa.

"Ah, that's better!" he sighed happily.

Just as the match was reaching half-time, Ella heard the sounds of cheering football crowds coming from the living room.

"Dad, does this mean you've finished my playhouse?" she asked, popping her head around the door.

"Ah, well now, um… I just came in to find some of my tools…" said Dad.

"I know exactly where your tool box is," said Ella. "Come with me and I'll show you."

Dad reluctantly followed her into the garage. There, on his work bench, was a big box of tools.

"Thank you, Ella," said Dad. "Now I'll be able to start building your playhouse."

"That's great!" said Ella. "I'll come back when you've finished!"

Dad carried his heavy box of tools down to the bottom of the garden.

"I suppose I can't put this off any longer!" he sighed to himself.

Rolling up his sleeves, he took out some tools and started building. For the rest of the afternoon, he hammered and sawed, screwed and painted, until, just as it was getting dark, he had finished the playhouse. It looked just like Ella's drawing!

"Ella will be so pleased!" Dad said to himself. "I'll go and tell her it's finished."

Wearily, he collected up his tools and carried the heavy box back to the house.

"I wonder where Ella is?" thought Dad.

He went into the living room, and there was Ella, fast asleep on the sofa.

"Ella," he called gently. "Wake up, Ella, your playhouse is finished!"

Ella slowly opened her eyes and yawned loudly.

"Dad," she said, "I've just had a lovely dream about a huge swimming pool in the garden! Please can you build me one of those now?"

No Time!

Jillian Harker

Autumn had come, and Scurry the squirrel was in a hurry. Yellow, orange and brown leaves were falling from the trees and piling up on the forest floor.

"Time to get busy," thought Scurry. "I must store some food for the winter." So Scurry scampered round under trees and bushes, hunting for nuts. Whenever he found some, he added them to the little pile under his tree. When the pile was big enough, he dug a hole and buried the nuts. All day long, Scurry rushed backwards and forwards. He had no time for anything else. He didn't even have time to see his friends.

"Hello, Scurry," called Milly Mouse, halfway through the morning. "I've been getting my winter bed ready."

"Hmm," mumbled Scurry, who wasn't really listening.

"It's a very good bed of comfortable dry leaves," said Milly. "I think it's my best winter bed ever. Would you like to come and see it?"

"No time!" muttered Scurry. "I'm in a hurry."

"Oh," said Milly sadly. She scurried away.

At lunchtime, Walter Woodpecker swooped down onto a branch of Scurry's tree. He tapped the trunk with his sharp beak to let Scurry know he was there.

"Guess what," Walter told his friend. "You know how I've been making holes in all the trees in the forest? Well, today I made my best, biggest hole ever. Do you want to come and see?"

"No time!" snapped Scurry. "I'm in a hurry."

"Oh," said Walter, sadly. He flew off.

Halfway through the afternoon, Rocky Rabbit hopped by.

"Scurry, my friend," he smiled. "I've been practising my digging. I've timed myself. I can dig a burrow faster than anyone in the forest. Why don't you come and watch me?"

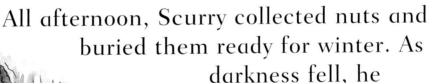

"No time!" yelled Scurry. "I'm in a hurry."

"Oh," sighed Rocky sadly. He hopped off.

"Doesn't anyone ever take any notice of what I say?" Scurry grumbled.

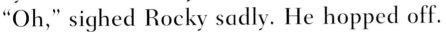

All afternoon, Scurry collected nuts and buried them ready for winter. As darkness fell, he scampered up his tree, into the hole near the top of the trunk, and curled up to sleep.

Not long afterwards, the wind began to blow. It whistled through the forest. The leaves on Scurry's tree shook. The wind tore them from the branches and whisked them away. Then it grew wilder. The branches creaked and groaned. Twigs snapped off and fell to the ground. The wind began to howl. It shook the whole tree, until Scurry woke with a start. What was happening? His house was moving. It was swaying from side to side. It felt as if it was going to...

CRASH! Over went the tree, and Scurry with it.

The wind stopped blowing. The forest was quiet. Scurry poked his nose out of his hole. His head hurt and his home was ruined. What was he going to do?

"Help! Help!" he called. There was a rustling noise, and Milly appeared.

"Who is it? What's the matter?" she asked, sleepily.

"It's me," whimpered Scurry. "My tree's been blown over. Where am I going to sleep?"

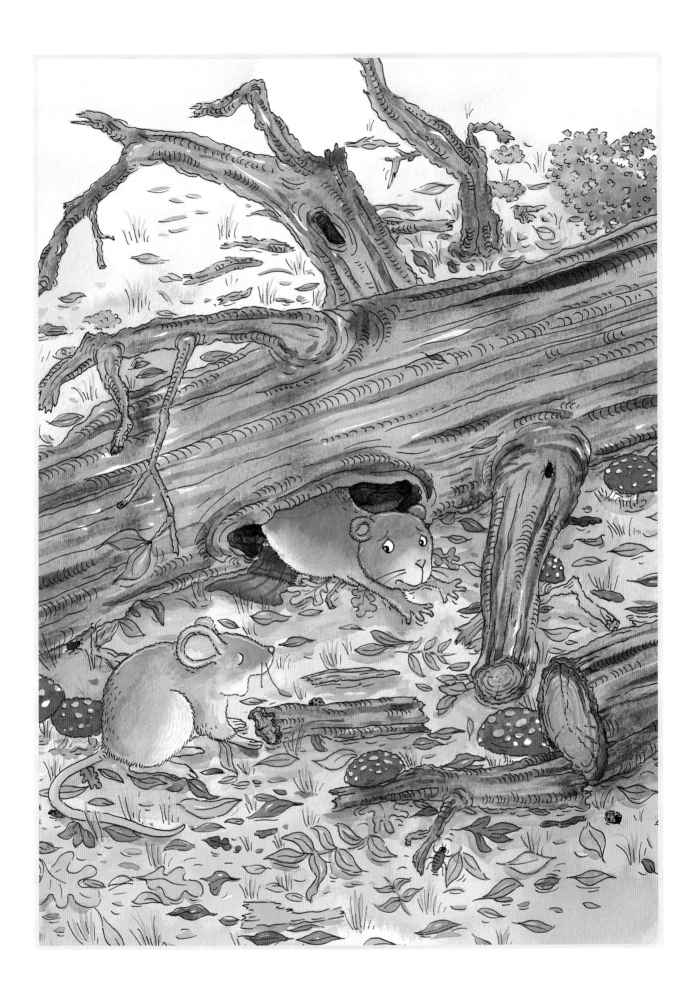

"Don't worry, Scurry," said Harriet. "Come and share my warm bed. It's tucked under that bush over there, safe from the wind. Come and see. There's plenty of room, and we'll sort things out in the morning."

"Thank you," said Scurry, quietly. He followed his friend.

Next morning, Scurry and Milly went to look at the damage.

"My lovely tree," sobbed Scurry. "Now I haven't got a home. Where would I find a comfortable hole like that again?"

"Easy!" said a voice. It was Walter.

"I told you I'd made a great hole. Come and see. It'll be perfect for you."

"Thank you," said Scurry, quietly. He followed his friend.

"You're right," said Scurry when he had tried the hole. "It's even better than my old home. But how am I going to get all the nuts from my winter store moved? It took me all day yesterday to bury them, and now I can't reach them, because my tree has fallen on top of them."

"No problem," said a voice. It was Rocky. "I can dig under that old tree in no time, get the nuts out, and carry them to your new home. Then I'll help you to dig a new store."

When the work was over,
Scruffy called his friends together.

"I want you all to come to tea with me," he told them.

"It's a thank you for helping me."

"Sorry," said Milly and Walter and Rocky all together.
"No time! We're in a hurry."

Scurry hung his head. Then the three friends burst out laughing.

"Oh, Scurry," they said. "We're not in a hurry. For a friend, we've always got time."